# The Smiley Snowman

M Christina Butler    Tina Macnaughton

LITTLE TIGER PRESS
London

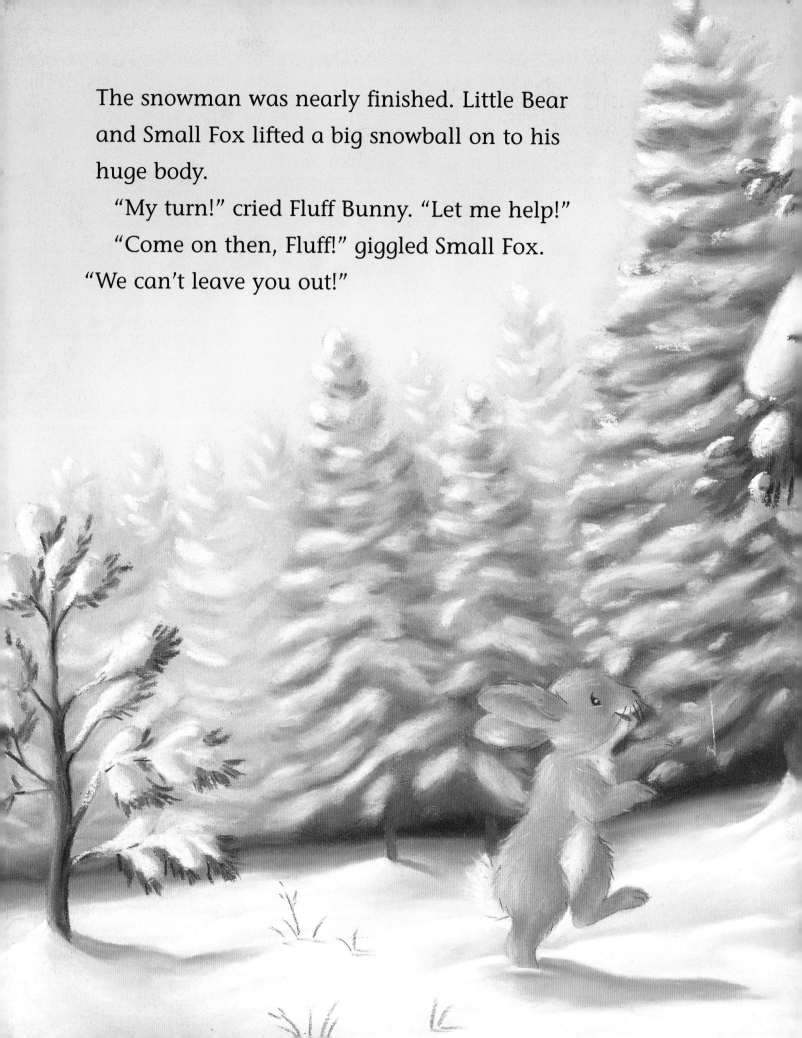

The snowman was nearly finished. Little Bear and Small Fox lifted a big snowball on to his huge body.

"My turn!" cried Fluff Bunny. "Let me help!"

"Come on then, Fluff!" giggled Small Fox. "We can't leave you out!"

"Here we go!" cried Little Bear, lifting
him up, and Fluff gave the snowman
a great, big smile.

"Yippee!" squeaked Fluff. "He looks
really happy now! Hello, Snowman!"

"Let's go, Fluff!" shrieked Little Bear and
Small Fox, sliding down the hill.
   "But what about Snowman?" Fluff called.
"Don't worry, Snowman, I'll stay with
   you. What shall we play?"

So together they played snowballs . . .

. . . and Fluff showed the snowman how to do headstands.

Then he told stories until the sky grew dark and snowflakes began to fall.

One by one, tiny lights started twinkling
in the valley below.

"I have to go now," said Fluff. "Night-
night, Snowman. See you tomorrow!"

Next morning the new snow sparkled bright.
"Wait for me!" gasped Fluff as he bounced
up the hill after Little Bear and Small Fox.
But the snowman looked sad and shivery.

"Oh no!" whispered Fluff. "What's wrong?"

"He looks cold to me," said Little Bear.

"He needs a hat!"

"I'll get a scarf!" cried Small Fox.

And off they went to see what they could find.

"This will warm him up!" giggled Little Bear
as they pulled the woolly hat and scarf
into place.

"What's happened to Fluff?" asked
Small Fox when they'd finished.
"I don't know," replied Little Bear.
"But there's something very strange
coming up the hill! Look!"

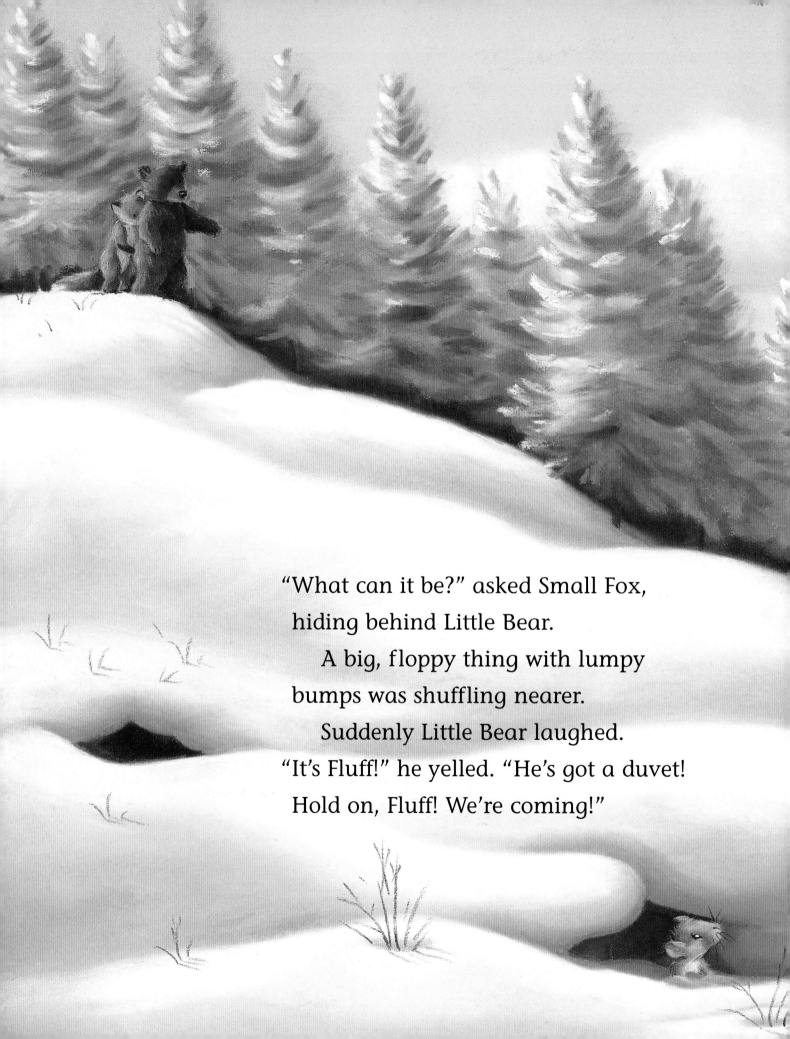

"What can it be?" asked Small Fox,
hiding behind Little Bear.

A big, floppy thing with lumpy
bumps was shuffling nearer.

Suddenly Little Bear laughed.
"It's Fluff!" he yelled. "He's got a duvet!
Hold on, Fluff! We're coming!"

Together the friends pulled the duvet
up to the snowman. Then they tucked
it round . . . and pulled it up . . . and
wrapped it round again . . .

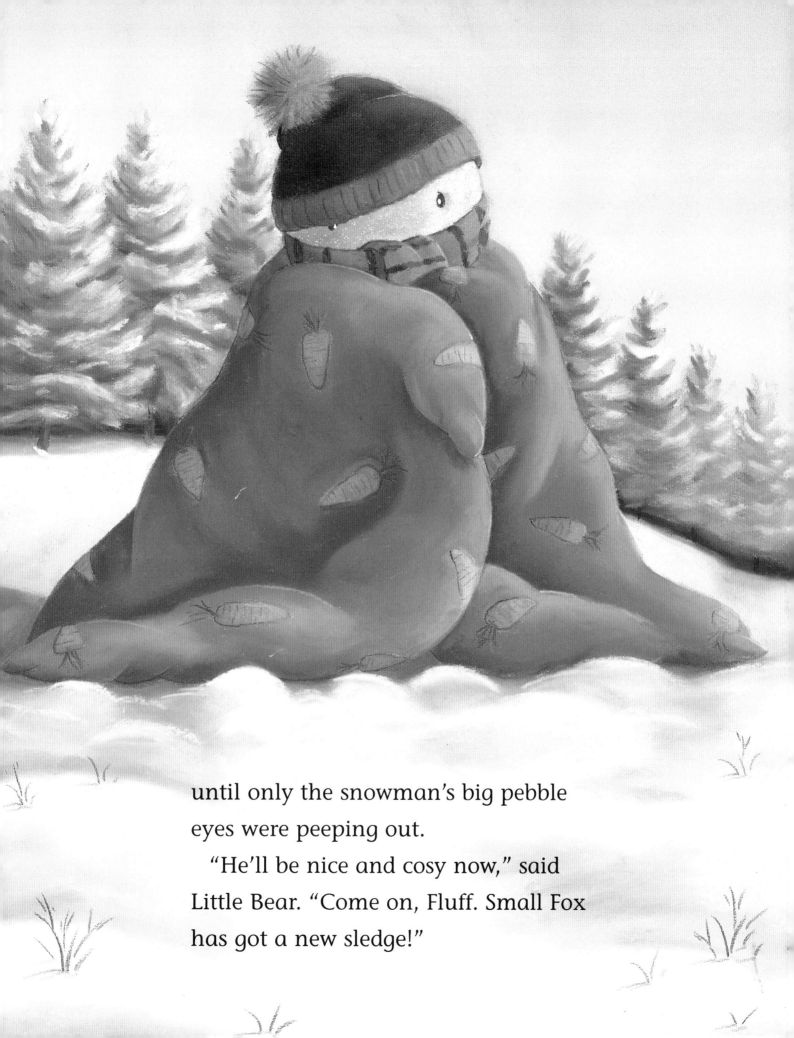

until only the snowman's big pebble
eyes were peeping out.

"He'll be nice and cosy now," said
Little Bear. "Come on, Fluff. Small Fox
has got a new sledge!"

Soon they were skimming
down the hill . . .

"We'll pull you, Fluff,"
laughed Little Bear. "Let's
go and see Snowman."

with snowball fights on the
way up — and down they
went again — until Fluff
was quite tired out and
flopped back on the sledge!

But something was wrong!

*Drip! Drip! Drip!* Drops of water were running down the snowman's face, and there were puddles of water everywhere!

"Our snowman's sinking!" Fluff yelled.

"He's melting!" cried Little Bear. "We'll have to make him cold again!"

They pulled off the duvet, and
threw his hat and scarf
in the air.
"Don't worry,
Snowman," cried
Fluff. "We'll save you!"

"More snow! More snow!"
shouted Little Bear as
they padded and
packed, and
smoothed and
patted.

Soon the snowman was bigger
and better than before.
"Wow!" gasped Little Bear.
"We nearly lost him!"
"But why does he still look
so *sad?*" puzzled Fluff, staring
up at the snowman.

Fluff stretched his arms as far as he could
around the snowman's big snow body.
"What's wrong, Snowman?" he asked
gently. "Please don't be so sad."
"Look," whispered Small Fox.
"Something is happening . . ."

"He's smiling!" cried Little Bear suddenly.

"Fluff's done it!" shouted Small Fox.

"Snowman wasn't cold on the outside. He was cold on the inside!" Fluff grinned. "He just needed a hug!"

And as the stars twinkled in the clear night sky, they gave the snowman another hug and his happy smile grew bigger than ever!